Waterman's Child

Waterman's Child

Barbara Mitchell
illustrated by Daniel San Souci

LOTHROP, LEE & SHEPARD BOOKS
New York

My great-grandma married a waterman at St. John's on the Bay when the Bay was brimming with oyster boats and wind-filled sails reached for the sky like flocks of snowy gulls.

While Great-grandpa sailed the Chesapeake on the *Mamie Mister*, pulling in oysters as wide as a waterman's hand, Great-grandma tended the house down on Chicken Point Road. She washed their clothes on the board, and scrubbed the floor with sand, and waited for news of the Tilghman dredge boats, gone in the storms for weeks.

"Oyster boats're in!" the schoolchildren cried, and everyone ran to the harbor. There was "Chip Beef Chicken" for supper that night, Great-grandpa's favorite.

In springtime, when Great-grandpa's nets bulged with herring and shad, Great-grandma rowed to Devil's Island to see the silvery catch. A thousand herring, five hundred shad!

Great-grandma and Great-grandpa watched their fish being packed—the old way, in barrels with plenty of salt.

Jacob and Anna Elizabeth watched the shipwright carve trail boards with his penknife, all the while spinning stories of swift-sailing log canoes: *Sweet Potatoe, Little Joe, The Frog,* and the beautiful *Island Bride.*

"A Tilghman-built boat is a proud-built boat," Great-grandpa used to say.

Summers, Anna Elizabeth and Jacob searched the tall grasses for soft-shell crabs. The crabs played games of hide-and-seek. Never mind that, there were always enough for supper—sizzling, crunchy, golden brown in Great-grandma's frying pan.

When the steamboat arrived with Baltimore folk, Great-grandpa piled their suitcases onto his wagon, along with supplies and the mail. The visitors trailed behind, helping themselves to summer fruit, breathing in the fresh island air. Belle, the old horse, knew just where to lead them: around to Miss Lizzie's boardinghouse at the end of Doctor's Road.

Great-grandma cooked for the boarders. Oh, the platters of crab cakes! Oh, the kettles of spicy crab soup! And Anna Elizabeth—my grandma—sat at the kitchen table, whackin' claws.

"When I grow up," my grandma told her mother, "I am going to marry a waterman, just like you."

"When I grow up," said Jacob, "I am going to be a waterman."

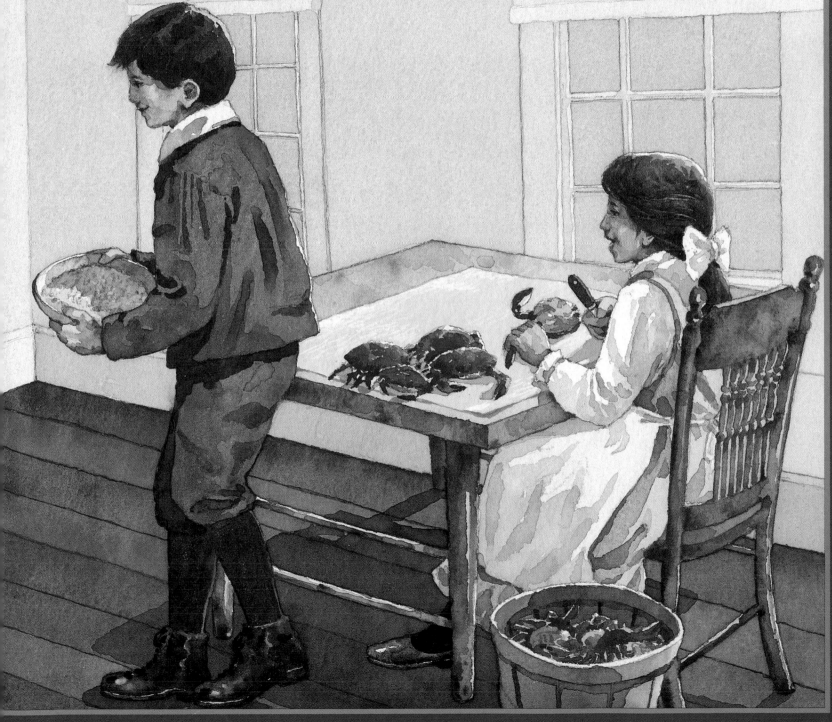

GRANDMA MARRIED A WATERMAN at St. John's on the Bay in the awful winter of '34, when icebreakers roamed the Bay.

When Betty Ann was a baby, Grandma says, the Choptank River froze over with ice fourteen inches thick. Grandpa oystered through holes in the ice, dragging a rake over the river bottom until the oysters were caught. A Chevy with a sled attached whisked the oysters over the frozen river to the Tilghman Packing Company.

"Crew took forty bushels," Grandpa told Grandma. "There'll be coins jingling in pockets this week."

Grandma baked Betty Ann's first birthday cake with the last of her sugar, and Grandpa invited the neighbors in.

Miss Ellen brought an applesauce cake. Captain Lou baked his sweet potato pie. The talk was all about oysters.

"Sure hope there's a market," the captain said.

"We'll make do," said Grandma.

"Always have," said Great-grandma, as Grandpa tuned his fiddle and feet

began to tap.

Summers, Grandma wrapped crab cakes at the packinghouse. Betty Ann and Thomas Jr. helped Grandpa set trotlines for crabbing. "No place I'd rather be," said Grandpa, "than out on Harris Creek come summer."

Then came the war. On Saturdays, everyone traipsed to Miss Mary's store. Grandpa joined in the watermen's talk, all of hard times, and oystering going bad, and skipjacks sitting idle in the marshes, and then of watermen sailing battleships far across the sea.

Grandma bought coffee with her precious ration stamps, while Thomas Jr. and Betty Ann—my mama—studied the candy: jelly beans, lemon drops, and candy sticks.

"A penny's worth," Mama told Miss Mary, and dropped the change from her nickel into the jar for watermen's families in need.

"She does her daddy proud," Miss Mary said. My grandma squeezed my mama's hand.

"When I grow up," my mama said, "I am going to marry a waterman, just like you."

"When I grow up," said Thomas Jr., "I am going to be a waterman."

MAMA MARRIED A WATERMAN at St. John's on the Bay
when fishermen's nets brought up bottles and cans,
and oysters turned black from lack of air and buried
themselves in silt.

When Daddy goes out oystering on our workboat *Danny Boy*, Mama goes with him. While he lowers the heavy tongs, Mama does the culling, measuring and sorting the catch.

Mama shucks herself a sample. "Snap," she says, and throws the sick oyster back into the Bay.

Come springtime, the *Mamie* is piled high with loads of oyster shell.
Daddy shovels the shell onto a new oyster bed. The baby oysters will
grow plump and healthy, he hopes.

Every October, we have Tilghman Island Day. Carloads of visitors cross over our drawbridge. They watch the shipwright shape the bow for a proud-built Tilghman boat. "Made for my island bride," the boatbuilder explains.

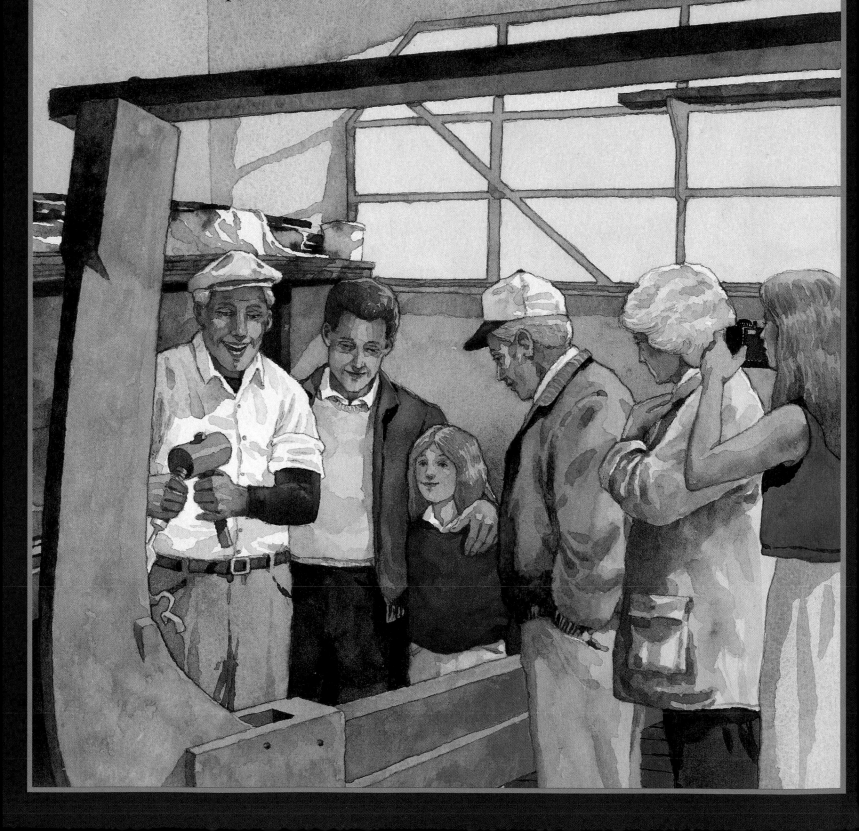

The visitors crowd Dogwood Harbor, where watermen tell about crabbing, fishing, and dredging and tonging for oysters. *Mamie Mister's* trail board gleams in the autumn sun.

"You can count the skipjacks on two hands now," Great-grandpa tells his audience.

Great-grandpa worries. The oyster catch is smaller every year. Will skipjacks sit idle again? Will oystering come to an end?

The firehouse bulges with seafood today. Oh, the platters of crab cakes! Oh, the kettles of spicy crab soup! Mama, Grandma, and Great-grandma cook all morning, then take a break to stroll around.

Danny shows off his crab buoy collection. I sell painted oyster shells from Devil's Island, where nothing else is left but a duck blind and an osprey's empty nest.

CRAB BUOYS
Not for sale

At the end of the day, when the visitors have gone, Mama and Daddy and Danny and I stroll down the road to St. John's on the Bay. We watch the sun set over the water and talk about our dreams. Mama dreams of writing a book about life on the water and all that it means. Daddy dreams of oysters as big as a waterman's hand. Danny dreams of a boat of his own.

I dream about going to college. About saving the oysters. About saving the Bay. "And then," I tell Mama, "I am going to marry a waterman at St. John's on the Bay."

Mama gives me a wink. "With dreams like those, Annie darlin'," she says, "good times are bound to return."

"Always have," I say.

For Amanda Rice
and Loren Manzione—
your heritage
—BJM

For Barbara Kouts
—DSS

The author and artist wish to thank the people of Tilghman Island,
without whose help this book could not have been done.
Although based on careful research, all characters in this story are fictional.

The illustrations in this book were done in watercolor.
The display and text type is Celestia Medium set on a Power Macintosh 7500/100.
Production supervision by Linda Palladino. Designed by Bea Jackson, Ivy Pages.

Text copyright © 1997 by Barbara Mitchell
Illustrations copyright © 1997 by Daniel San Souci
Lothrop, Lee & Shepard Books, a division of William Morrow & Company, Inc.,
1350 Avenue of the Americas, New York, New York 10019.
First Edition   1 2 3 4 5 6 7 8 9 10
Library of Congress Cataloging in Publication Data
Mitchell, Barbara.
Waterman's child / by Barbara Mitchell; illustrated by Daniel San Souci.
p. cm.
Summary: Young Annie begins with her great grandmother and tells about
her family's life as fishermen on Chesapeake Bay.
ISBN 0-688-10861-X. — ISBN 0-688-10862-8 (lib.bdg.)
[1. Fishers—Chesapeake Bay (Md. and Va.)—Fiction.
2. Oyster fisheries—Chesapeake Bay (Md. and Va.)—Fiction. 3. Chesapeake Bay (Md. and Va.)—Fiction.]
I. San Souci, Daniel, ill. II. Title. PZ7.M686Wat 1996 [Fic]—dc20 94-40734 CIP AC